Shhh!

PHILOMEL BOOKS

A division of Penguin Young Readers Group.

Published by The Penguin Group.

Penguin Group (USA) Inc., 375 Hudson Street, New York, NY 10014, U.S.A.

Penguin Group (Canada), 90 Eglinton Avenue East, Suite 700, Toronto,
Ontario M4P 2Y3, Canada (a division of Pearson Penguin Canada Inc.).

Penguin Books Ltd, 80 Strand, London WC2R 0RL, England.

Penguin Ireland, 25 St. Stephen's Green, Dublin 2, Ireland
(a division of Penguin Books Ltd).

Penguin Group (Australia), 250 Camberwell Road, Camberwell,
Victoria 3124, Australia (a division of Pearson Australia Group Pty Ltd).

Penguin Books India Pvt Ltd, 11 Community Centre, Panchsheel Park,
New Delhi - 110 017, India.

Penguin Group (NZ), 67 Apollo Drive, Rosedale, Auckland 0632,
New Zealand (a division of Pearson New Zealand Ltd).

Penguin Books (South Africa) (Pty) Ltd, 24 Sturdee Avenue,
Rosebank, Johannesburg 2196, South Africa.

Penguin Books Ltd, Registered Offices: 80 Strand,
London WC2R 0RL, England.

Edited by Tamra Tuller.   Design by Semadar Megged.
Text set in 19.5-Point Maiandra GD.
The illustrations are rendered in watercolors, gouache, and ink.

Library of Congress Cataloging-in-Publication Data
Gorbachev, Valeri. Shhh! / Valeri Gorbachev. p. cm. Summary: A little
boy tries hard to be quiet while his little brother takes a nap.
ISBN 978-0-399-25429-1 [1. Brothers—Fiction. 2. Naps (Sleep)—Fiction.
3. Noise—Fiction. 4. Play—Fiction.] I. Title. PZ7.G6475Sh 2011
[E]—dc22
2010041652.   ISBN 978-0-399-25429-1
10 9 8 7 6 5 4 3 2 1

Valeri Gorbachev

Snhh!

Philomel Books
An Imprint of Penguin Group (USA) Inc.

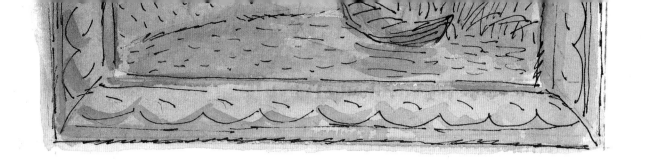

When my baby brother sleeps,
I am very quiet.
I don't jump around.
I don't ride my horse. I don't even sing.
I walk on my tippy-toes.

"Please stop laughing,"
I say to the clown.

"Please stop fighting,"
I tell the knights.

Shhh!

"Please don't growl so loud,"
I whisper to the tiger.

Shhh!

"Please don't fly your buzzing plane," I ask the pilot.

"Please stop your train," I beg the conductor.

"Please stop firing your cannons," I plead with the pirates.

When my baby brother sleeps,
it is so quiet in my house.
I can even hear a fly!

But when my baby
brother wakes up . . .

The clown begins to laugh

and the knights begin to fight.

The tiger starts growling

and the pilot's plane buzzes in the sky.

The train leaves the station
with a loud whistle

and the pirates fire their cannons.

And I am jumping and
shouting and singing again!
And I am playing my
trumpet and my drum
and riding my horse
around the house!

Until . . .

I am quiet again.

Because I love my baby brother so.